This book is dedicated to all of my real-life worry dolls.
Without your inspiration and support, this book and
so many other dreams would not have been possible.

- Allison Canale

www.mascotbooks.com

Ella and the Worry Doll

©2013 Allison Canale. All Rights Reserved. No part of this
publication may be reproduced, stored in a retrieval system
or transmitted in any form by any means electronic, mechanical,
or photocopying, recording or otherwise without the permission
of the author.

For more information, please contact:
Mascot Books
560 Herndon Parkway #120
Herndon, VA 20170
info@mascotbooks.com

CPSIA Code: PRT0813A
ISBN-10: 1620863324
ISBN-13: 9781620863329

Printed in the United States

Ella and the Worry Doll

Allison Canale

illustrated by Ingrid Lefebvre

MASCOT
BOOKS

Late one starry evening,
Ella sat straight up in bed.
Her troubled thoughts and worries
were all dancing through her head.

She tried so hard to calm her fears, they would not go away.
Her mother asked her what was wrong, she didn't want to say.

Mom asked Ella if friends at school were treating her alright.

Dad asked her if the slippers she was wearing were too tight.

Her brother thought a monster
may have made his sister scared.

And sister wondered
if it was from
stories that they shared.

Tired as she sat in bed, she could not fall asleep.
Thinking of her troubles, little Ella began to weep.

Ella's Noni had a thought;
she always had ideas.
She also had her share of worries
and doubts throughout the years.

"When I was just a little girl," her Noni said to Ella,
"I called upon a magic friend, a most amazing fella.
I told him of my greatest fears and things that made me scared.
He told me that he'd handle them; he really seemed to care."

Ella asked her Noni, "How do friends get rid of troubles?"
Noni replied, "If you believe, they'll float away like bubbles!"

Noni reached into her pocket and pulled out a little friend.
"Just whisper all your worries and they'll soon come to an end."

The little friend was seated upon Ella's bed nightstand.
She hoped the doll would help her just the way her Noni planned.
Ella looked into his face then closed her eyes so tight.
She whispered, "By tomorrow, you'll have made my night alright."

"I just know," said Ella,
"that this doll will calm my fears."
Then she lay back on her pillow
and she grinned from ear to ear.

When Ella thought of thunderstorms,
she imagined that her friend
Put cotton candy round the clouds
to make the loud noise end.

When Ella thought of spiders and slippery, slimy snakes,

Her friend attracted them away by offering them cakes.

Ella was convinced she heard
a monster's teeth go "crunch,"
But then she saw her little friend
just nibbling his lunch.

The little doll didn't say a word, but Ella still believed.
Then she thought about her worries, and she really felt relieved.
Snuggling in her comfy bed, she heard a bubble pop.
Then calming feelings floated down, and off to sleep she dropped.

In the morning, Noni asked if Ella had exciting news.
"I'm feeling better, Noni!" She no longer had the blues!

"You know, my little Ella, how your worries came to end?
It's because you just believed and told your tiny, little friend."

Ella was so thankful and she couldn't help but smile.
And to this day, she asks her doll for help once in a while.

Ella shares her caring friend
with all who might be worried.
Because she knows
her friend will help
and do it in a hurry.

So if you might be carrying
a troubled thought or two.
Just tell this friend and then believe,
and surely he'll help you!

About the Author

Allison Canale has taught young children for over twenty years. Establishing two preschools and an infant care center, she has had the privilege of meeting and connecting with hundreds of students and their families. A proud mother of three grown children, Allison currently lives in Rutland, Massachusetts, enjoying outdoor activities including gardening, hiking, and biking with her loving husband, Michael.